How to CATCH SANTA

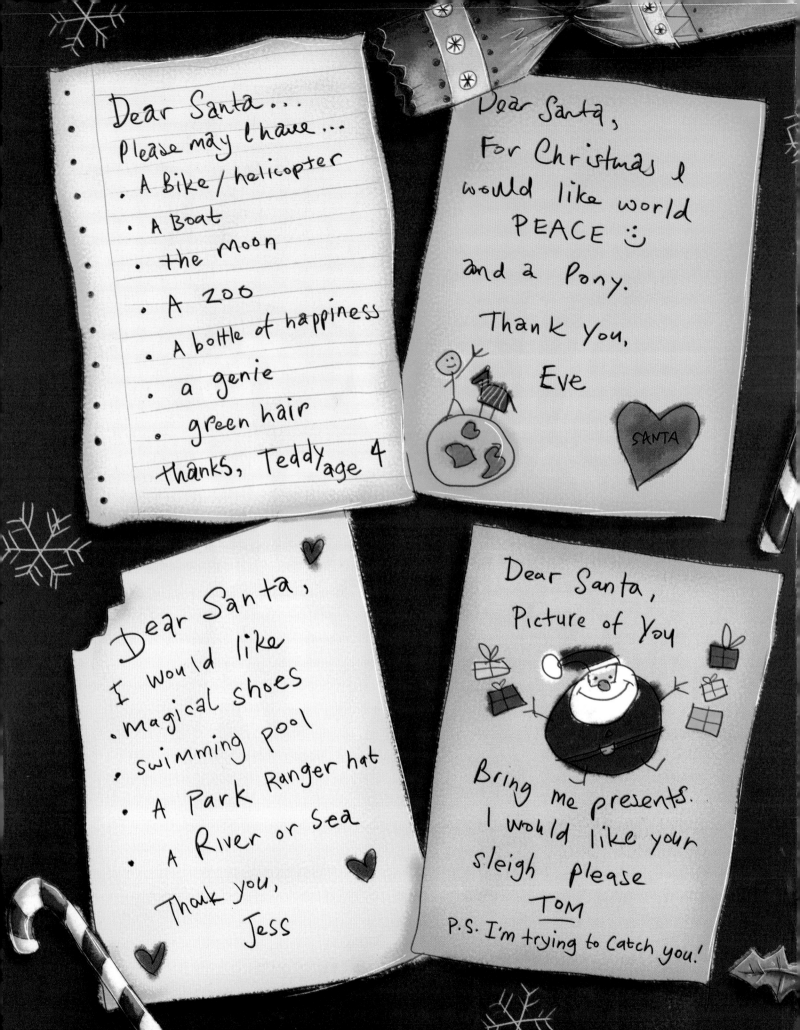

Dear Santa...
Please may I have...
· A Bike / helicopter
· A Boat
· the moon
· A zoo
· A bottle of happiness
· a genie
· green hair
thanks, Teddy age 4

Dear Santa,
For Christmas I would like world PEACE ☺ and a Pony.
Thank you,
Eve

SANTA

Dear Santa,
I would like
· magical shoes
· swimming pool
· A Park Ranger hat
· A River or Sea
Thank you,
Jess

Dear Santa,
Picture of You

Bring me presents. I would like your sleigh please
TOM
P.S. I'm trying to catch you!

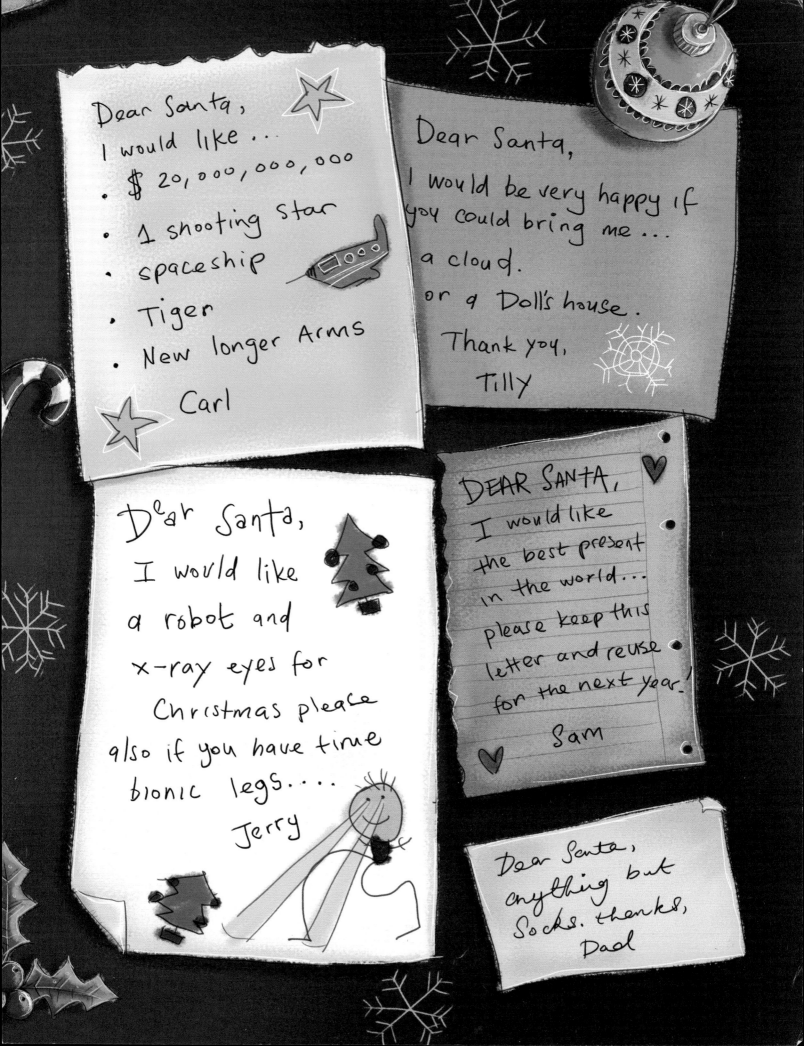

How to Catch Santa

BY JEAN REAGAN   ILLUSTRATED BY LEE WILDISH

SCHOLASTIC INC.

For my niece, Judy, and for all my hiking
and critique buddies. Thank you! —J.R.

Merry Christmas, Ivy, Oscar, Grace, and Laura —L.W.

ISBN 978-1-338-33935-2

12 11 10 9 8 7 6 5 4 3 2 1   18 19 20 21 22 23

Printed in the U.S.A.   40

First Scholastic printing, September 2018

The text of this book is set in Goudy Old Style.
The illustrations were created digitally.

After waiting for days and days and *days*, it's finally Christmas Eve.

And *that's* when you can try to catch Santa.

As you know, Santa's very busy, and you won't be able to keep him for long. So plan ahead. Figure out *now* how to make the most of your time.

First of all, don't you have a zillion questions to ASK him?

QUESTIONS FOR SANTA:

How do you squeeze down chimneys?

How do you stay clean?

What about houses with no chimneys?

How fast do reindeer fly to get everywhere in one night?

What's their fuel? Magic?

Do elves ever sneak a ride in your sleigh?
What about kids?

How do you find kids who are away on trips?

What's *your* favorite toy?

Do you get mountains and **mountains** of letters?

Who invents new toys
at your workshop?

The elves?

Mrs. Claus?

You?

Do you really eat cookies at everyone's house?

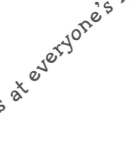

Maybe you have things you want to TELL him.

THINGS TO TELL SANTA:

I'm trying very hard to be good.
My sister is, too, even if it doesn't look like it.

Thank you Santa.

Thank you for the presents!
Sorry I always forget to send a thank-you note.

I know what my mom and dad want.
They were too busy to write to you.

And maybe you have things you want to GIVE him.
(Santa will *love* that!)

THINGS TO GIVE
SANTA:

A headlamp for going
down dark, dark chimneys

A nose warmer for
cold sleigh rides

Drawings of
Santa with
your family

Homemade Christmas
decorations for Mrs. Claus

Okay, now you know what you'll do once you catch Santa.
It's time to figure out HOW to do it. Definitely don't try
anything too WILD AND CRAZY:

Lassoing Santa

Distracting him with a giant candy cane

Luring him into a snow trap

Tying nets between palm trees

Instead: Be crafty! Be clever! Be *gentle*!

If you're very lucky, you will *actually catch Santa*. But you might only catch a *glimpse* of him. Or you might just find "Santa's been here" clues.

PLAN FOR ALL THESE POSSIBILITIES:

Early on Christmas Eve, write Santa a note and fill it with glitter.

When he opens it, glitter will sprinkle all over him and he'll leave a trail. That's a "Santa's been here" clue for sure.

Scatter carrots in your yard or on the windowsill.

If they disappear, that's a "reindeer have been here" clue!

CARROTS

Write Santa riddles, but
DON'T GIVE THE ANSWERS! (Yet.)

Bake him cookies.

Instead of putting them by the tree, draw arrows leading to your room.

String bells and chimes above the cookies.

That way, he'll make a racket and wake you up.

Now try to be patient. While you wait, sing Christmas songs and read books about Santa. Maybe you'll even get some new Santa-catching ideas.

Ask your mom and dad if they ever tried to catch Santa when they were little. Do they have any tricks? Check with your grandma and grandpa, too.

When it starts to get dark, Santa and his reindeer begin their rounds. Have everyone keep an eye out the window.

If your family makes lots of noise—laughing, eating, talking, playing games—say "*Shhhhhh!*" every now and then and listen for Santa sounds. . . .

SANTA SOUNDS:

Santa doing stretches
on your neighbor's roof

Sleigh bells

"Ho, Ho, HO!"

Reindeer whinnying
in the distance

Elves giggling

When you start to get sleepy,
MAKE LAST-MINUTE PREPARATIONS:

Leave the Christmas tree lights on
to help Santa see his way around.

Rudolph-with-his-nose-so-bright can't help him from the roof.

Set out your Santa riddles with a note that says "For help with the answers, wake me up."

Santa won't be able to resist!

Is your puppy a good watchdog? A good, *gentle* watchdog? If yes, then let him stay in your bedroom.

Remember, Santa won't come to your house until you're asleep.

Before you lay your head on your pillow, peek out the window one last time.

Good luck catching Santa, and . . .

MERRY CHRISTMAS!

And if you didn't catch Santa this time,
don't worry. There's always next year. . . .

you,
–A

g me

azing

…

next

Dear Santa,
I wish you a lovely Christmas.

thank you very much for all the fantastic presents.

Thanks

To SANTA
I like your beard.

Thank you for the presents.

To SANTA,
I want to thank you for my presents. My cat likes his too. Here is a drawing of him.

To SANTA

Thank you for my beautiful presents

Thanks for all the socks, Santa.
Dad

JEAN REAGAN was born in Alabama but spent most of her childhood in Japan. She now lives in Salt Lake City with her husband. In the summers, they serve as backcountry volunteers in Grand Teton National Park in Wyoming.

LEE WILDISH became interested in art at a very young age. He is the illustrator of many acclaimed children's books and has also worked in advertising and greeting card design. Lee lives in Nottinghamshire, England.

■ SCHOLASTIC

www.scholastic.com

ISBN 978-1-338-35517-8

$5.99 US

50599

9 781338 355178